Spotlight on Charity

A Story About Overcoming Selfishness

Featuring the Psalty family of characters
created by Ernie and Debby Rettino

Written by Ken Gire
Illustrated by John Dickenson,
Matt Mew, and Bob Payne

From Focus on the Family Publishing/Maranatha! for Kids
Pomona, CA 91799. Distributed by Word Books, Waco, Texas.

Library of Congress Catalog Card Number 87-80940
ISBN 084-9999-995

"Attention, Churchmouse Choir," Charity Churchmouse shouted above the hubbub of excited, squeaky mice voices. The group quieted down to listen to their leader.

"I'm so glad you have all come back for another year of choir," Charity began.

"Who's going to sing the solo this year?" Limburger interrupted Charity.

"We'll have tryouts and give everyone a chance," Charity answered patiently.

"Who's going to play piano?" another choir member asked.

"I don't know," Charity replied. "We'll find someone."

Little did Charity know that her enemy, sneaky, slinky
Risky Rat, was hiding in the shadows listening in.

"Aha!" Risky said to himself. "She needs a piano
player? How perfectly sublime! To pass this up would be a
crime! I'll disguise myself and turn the sweet Miss Charity
Churchmouse into a selfish monster. *And* I'll ruin the church
program!"

Soon Risky Rat was twirling a cane and strutting up to Charity, who had begun to practice singing ''Jesus Loves Me.''

''Excuse me for interrupting such a great talent . . .'' Risky Rat began.

''Why thank you,'' Charity responded with a giggle. ''Have we met before? You look kind of familiar.''

"Allow me to introduce myself," Risky offered. He removed his hat and gave her one of his business cards. "I'm the Piano Man. I play the keys just as you please."

"Did you say *Piano* Man?" asked Charity.

"At your service night and day, I'll play the piano, you name the pay."

"You're hired!" announced Charity, shaking hands with him. "Would you please play along as I choose music for the solo tryouts?"

"Tryouts?" Risky Rat asked with surprise. "Don't waste your time with tryouts, mousey dear. Why, you're whiskers and tails better than any singer here." As he spoke, he slyly whirled his greasy whiskers between his fingers.

"Do you really think so?" Charity's eyes were big with amazement and pleasure.

"A nightingale never sang as sweetly!" he said, with a mischievous grin.

Charity blushed. ''But, but I wanted to give everyone a chance to try out.''

Risky Rat took the music for ''Jesus Loves Me'' and scratched out the words. Then, with a few flicks of his pen, he rewrote the song. ''Here, sing this, sweetie, and you be the judge.''

Charity took the music and began to sing.
"How I love me.
This is so,
And I'm meant
to sing solo.
You can hear,
my voice is best,
Better far than all the rest.
Oh, how I love me.
Oh, how I love me.
Oh, how I love me.
I'm meant to sing solo."

"Don't you sound simply marvelous?" Risky Rat asked with a phoney smile that reached from ear to ear.

"You're right! I'm the one to sing the solo!" Charity answered, not noticing his fake smile.

Charity then called together all the mice and made her announcement. "No use wasting valuable time trying to decide on a soloist. I will perform the solo this year. The rest of you can hum along in the background."

Limburger sighed in disappointment. Everyone's whiskers drooped and shoulders sagged.

"And I promise you," Charity continued, "when I get to be a big star, I'll always remember all the little church mice who were with me at the beginning."

From that moment on, Risky Rat worked even harder to make Charity a selfish singing star. First he had her pose for photos to hand out to all her fans after her great solo.

Then he suggested, "Let's send out invitations for your performance to everyone we can think of."

Everyday he encouraged Charity to practice and practice and practice for long hours.

During one session, Risky sat on the piano bench and said, "Sing along as I play. Do, Re, Me."

"Do, Re, Me," sang Charity.

"Me, me, me," continued the rat.

"Me, me, me," echoed Charity.

"Ah, my favorite word," Risky muttered under his breath as Charity continued to sing.

Finally the day of the big program came. Risky Rat issued orders to everyone. "Polish the piano. Dust the pews. Get them ready to use. Find the candles and the matches. Separate the music into batches. You there, Limburger! Climb up to the rafters. Man the spotlight—don't mind the height! Make sure the light is focused where our new star, Charity, will sit when it's time for her solo."

The mice hustled and bustled about so much that their whiskers went limp and their tails began to drag. But they carried out all of Risky's orders.

By evening, everything was in its proper place, properly
scrubbed, and properly polished. Even the Churchmouse
Choir looked squeaky clean as the group filed in to stand
behind the piano. They nervously watched as the audience
got bigger and bigger.

"Look at all the people!" one of them mumbled.

Then, as the Piano Man softly played a song, Charity
strode onto the stage. She smiled at the audience, and a hush
filled the room.

Charity took her position on the piano. Limburger, who had climbed high up in the rafters, switched the spotlight on just as Charity opened her mouth to sing.

"Oh, no!" Limburger moaned. The spotlight was not focused on Charity! He quickly tried to adjust it, but as he did, the light jerked back and forth.

Charity slid all over the piano top, trying to stay in the spotlight. She glared angrily up into the rafters.

When Limburger saw how mad Charity was, he got nervous and lost his footing. "Help!" he wailed. His little paws grabbed for the spotlight handle. Thankfully, his grasp held, and he was saved from a great plunge.

But his attempt to save himself made the light shift far to the right. Charity scooted over once again to stay in the spotlight.

"Eeek!" Charity shrieked. She had slid too close to the piano's edge. Losing her balance, she tumbled right into the belly of the piano!

The audience roared with laughter.

Charity tried to keep singing her solo from inside the piano, but some of the key hammers bopped her on the head. As they did, they produced flat notes.

Meanwhile, Risky Rat kept playing, loving every minute of Charity's disgrace. The Churchmouse Choir, not knowing what else to do, started to sing the song where Charity's voice had trailed off.

Risky Rat, surprised that the choir mice had saved the day, became flustered. "Oh man, oh man! This wasn't in my plan!"

He pounded hard on the piano keys in his frustration. As he did, Charity went flying into the air.

With a PLOP, she landed right in the middle of the Churchmouse Choir. Dusting herself off, she joined in the singing.

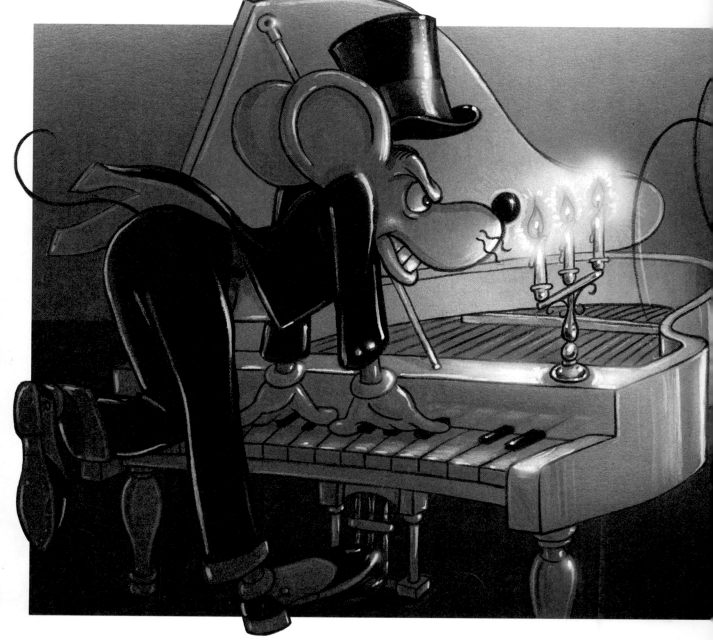

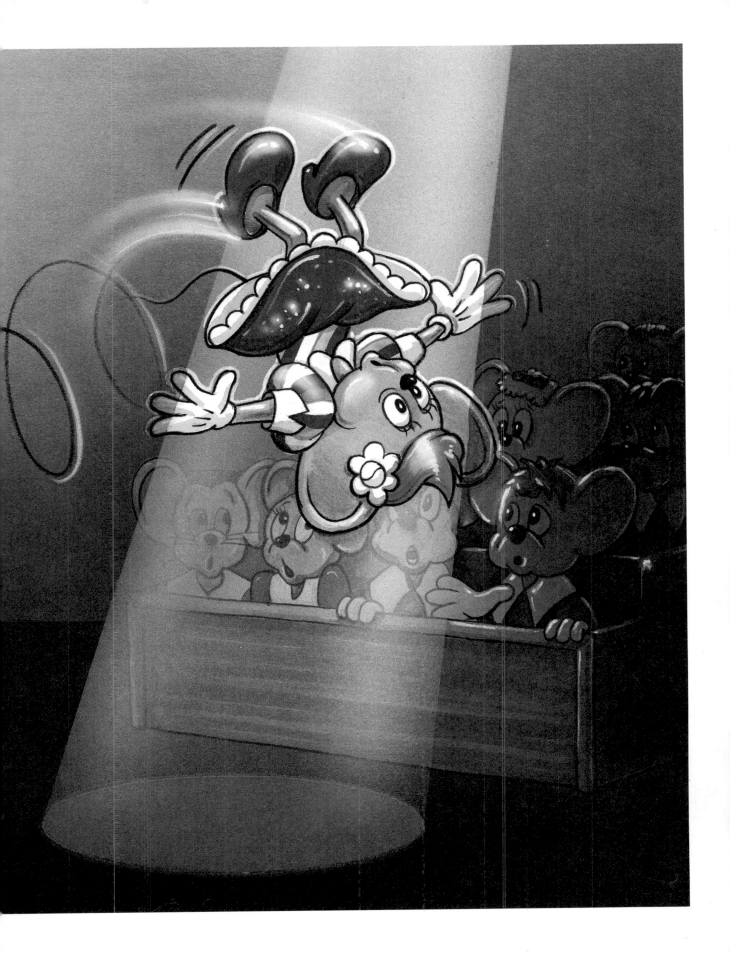

When the song ended, the audience stood up and clapped. Everyone thought the program was wonderful.

Charity and the choir members smiled at the crowd and felt pleased with themselves. Glancing over at the Piano Man, Charity noticed he was bowing as though he deserved all the credit for the fine performance.

Then Charity remembered that she had known the Piano Man before, but by a different name. ''You're not the Piano Man!'' she exclaimed. ''You're Risky Rat!''

''It *is* Risky Rat!'' someone called out.

The audience started to boo.

''Is that so? Well, watch me go!'' huffed Risky, turning on his heel as the audience booed him from the church.

Then Charity announced to the whole church: "I...I...I want to say I'm sorry. I thought the Piano Man was trying to help me, but I didn't know he was really Risky Rat. Risky tricked me.

"I'm sorry for being so selfish," Charity continued. "I didn't even give anyone else a chance to try out for the solo."

At this point Charity started to cry. One of the choir mice took a hanky out of her pocket and handed it to Charity, who daintily blew her nose.

As Charity stuffed the hanky into her own pocket, she went on: "I was not very loving to all of you. I know love is not selfish, but I got caught up in thinking only of myself. Can you forgive me?"

Some of the mice came over to Charity and told her they forgave her. Others said they had a hard time not being selfish and unloving, too. Limburger managed to climb all the way down from the rafters, and he hugged Charity.

Then, with their arms around each other, everyone in the church sang "Jesus Loves Me"—this time with the *right* words.